THE USBORNE
FIRST
COOKBOOK

Angela Wilkes
Illustrated by Stephen Cartwright

New edition edited by Fiona Watt and designed by Rachel Kirkland

with thanks to Anne Civardi

Before you start

Before you begin, read through the recipe you are going to cook and make sure that you have everything you need. If you are not sure of some of the equipment you need to use, or some of the cooking words in the recipe pages 70-71 will help you.

All the recipes in this book are for four people.

Ingredients

At the beginning of each recipe you'll find a list of all its ingredients. Weigh any dry ingredients on kitchen scales and measure liquids in a measuring jug. Cut or slice any ingredients you need to, before you start to cook.

Wipe mushrooms and slice them finely.

Chop onions as finely as you can.

Peel a clove of garlic before you crush it.

Your oven

Cook things on the middle shelf of your oven unless the recipe says something different. Move the shelves to the right position before you start cooking.

Switch on your oven to the temperature given in the recipe so that it has heated up by the time you use it. If you have a fan oven you will need to use a lower heat. Look in its instruction book to find out how much lower it needs to be.

Do not start cooking unless there is an adult there to help you.

2

Things to remember

Be careful

Be very careful when you use a sharp knife. Always cut on a chopping board. Put hot dishes on a wooden board or a heat-proof mat, not straight onto a work surface or table.

Turn saucepan handles to the side of your cooker so that you do not knock them off. Never leave the kitchen while electric or gas rings are on.

Follow the recipe

Don't be tempted to open the oven door while things are cooking unless the recipe tells you to, or you think something may be burning.

Stay clean

Always put on oven gloves before picking up anything hot, or when you are putting things into or taking them out of your oven.

Try to stay as clean as you can while you're cooking. Wear an apron and roll up your sleeves. If you spill anything wipe it up at once.

Remember to turn off your oven when you have finished cooking.

Surprise baked tomatoes

INGREDIENTS

4 large tomatoes
4 eggs
salt and pepper
1 tablespoon chopped
parsley

Use the biggest tomatoes you can find for this. If you are very hungry cook two tomatoes each.

Cut a small slice off the top of each tomato and scoop out the pulp with a spoon. Season inside the tomatoes with salt and pepper.

Oven setting:180°C/350°F/ Gas mark 4

Grease a shallow, ovenproof baking dish with margarine or butter on kitchen paper.

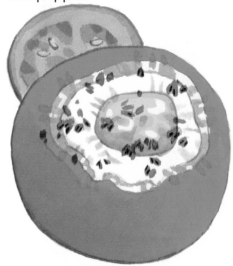

Put the tomatoes in the dish and break an egg into each one. Season the eggs with a little salt and sprinkle parsley on top.

Put the tops on the tomatoes and bake them in the oven for about 20 minutes until the eggs have set.

Eat the tomatoes while they are hot with lots of crusty bread and butter.

Welsh rarebit

Mix the cheese, mustard, egg, Worcestershire sauce and a pinch of salt and pepper together in a bowl.

Put the slices of bread under the grill and toast them on one side only.

Spread the cheese mixture thickly over the untoasted sides of the bread and put the slices of tomato on top.

Put the toast back under the grill until the cheese is bubbly and light brown. Put it on a warm plate and eat straight away.

Cheese and herb dip

INGREDIENTS

350g (12oz) cream cheese
150g (5floz) single cream
2 finely chopped spring
   onions
2 tablespoons of fresh
   chopped parsley
2 tablespoons of fresh
   chopped chives
2 teaspoons of chopped
   mint
1 crushed clove garlic
a squeeze of lemon juice

Mix the cream into the cheese. The mixture should be light, but stiff enough to hold its shape.

Mix in the onion, herbs, lemon juice and seasoning. Taste it and add more salt, pepper or herbs if you like.

Prepare the vegetables. Peel the carrots and cucumber and trim the celery. Cut them all into finger-length sticks.

Spoon the dip into a dish and push the vegetables into it.

Hot herb bread

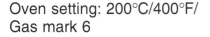

INGREDIENTS

1 French loaf
90g (3oz) softened
    butter
2 crushed cloves of garlic
    (if you like)
1 tablespoon of fresh
    chopped parsley
1 tablespoon of fresh
    chopped chives

Oven setting: 200°C/400°F/
Gas mark 6

Mix the butter, herbs and garlic together.

Make cuts along the loaf but do not cut right through it.

Spread both sides of each cut with herb butter.

Wrap the loaf in foil. Bake it for 10-15 minutes.

Eat the bread hot. It tastes wonderful with salad.

Leek and tomato soup

Peel and dice the potatoes.

Spoon the tomatoes into a jug of boiling water. Leave them for a minute, then fish them out.

It will now be easy to peel the skin off the tomatoes. Chop them up roughly.

Trim off the tops and roots of the leeks and peel away the tough outer layer. Cut the leeks in half lengthways and rinse them well in cold water. Slice them quite finely.

Gently melt the butter in a big, thick-based saucepan. Add the leeks, stir them and cook them slowly until soft.

Add the chopped tomatoes. Stir them into the leeks and let them cook slowly until their juice starts to run.

Add the potato, a pinch of salt, water and sugar. Put a lid on the pan and let the soup simmer for about 20 minutes until the vegetables are cooked.

Take the pan off the heat. To make the soup smooth, push it through a sieve or put it in a blender, if you have an adult to help you.

Pour the soup back into the pan and reheat it gently. Taste it and add more seasoning if you like.

Stir the cream into the soup and serve it at once.

9

Omelette

The fresher the eggs are, the better they taste.

INGREDIENTS

2 eggs
a knob of butter
salt and pepper

Omelettes are very quick to make. You can make a plain omelette or add one of the fillings below.

Break the eggs into a bowl. Add a pinch of salt and pepper and beat the eggs lightly.

Try one of these tasty fillings, or think up one of your own. You only need to use a little filling.

a little grated cheese

chopped tomato cooked in butter

a tablespoonful of chopped parsley and chives

chopped, cooked bacon or pieces of sliced ham

Melt the butter in a small frying pan and swirl it around. When it foams, pour in the eggs.

When the omelette begins to set around the edges, add your filling.

Pull the edges of the omelette gently into the middle with a fork and tilt the pan to let the runny egg flow to the sides to cook.

When the top of the omelette has set but is still creamy, loosen the edges and fold it over. Slip it straight onto a plate.

Eat the omelette straight away while it is hot. If there are lots of you, make an omelette for each person.

Eggy bread

Not all things take a long time to cook. Some of the nicest things are very quick to make - like eggy bread. You can make it for breakfast or for tea.

INGREDIENTS
4 thick slices of white
   bread with the crusts
   cut off
4 eggs
60g (2½oz) butter
2 tablespoons oil
salt and pepper

Break the eggs into a dish and beat them well. Season with a pinch of salt and pepper.

Take care

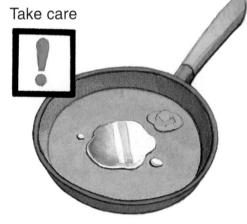

Heat the butter and oil in a frying pan. It should be hot but not smoking.

Dip the slices of bread in the egg. Let any extra egg drip back into the dish.

Fry the slices of bread on both sides until they are crisp and golden brown. Eat eggy bread while it is hot. Sprinkle it with salt or a little sugar, if you like.

Stuffed jacket potatoes

INGREDIENTS

4 large well-scrubbed
    potatoes
50g (2oz) butter
75g (3oz) chopped ham
75g (3oz) grated cheese
a little milk
1 tablespoon chopped
    parsley
salt and black pepper

Oven setting; 200°C/400°F/
Gas mark 6

Prick the potatoes with a fork.
Put them on a baking tray and
bake them for 1-1½ hours.

Push a skewer into the biggest
potato. If it is soft, it is cooked.
If it is hard, cook it a little
longer.

When the potatoes are cooked,
cut them in half lengthways and
scoop out the middles.

Mash the potato in a bowl. Add
the rest of the ingredients and
mix everything together well.

Fill the potato skins with the
mixture and bake them for
another 15 minutes. Decorate
with parsley.

Stuffed eggs

INGREDIENTS

as many eggs as you
like
mayonnaise
salt and pepper
finely chopped parsley

Put the eggs in a saucepan of cold water. Bring the water to the boil, then let it simmer for ten minutes.

This stops a black ring from forming around the yolks.

Take the pan off the heat and put it under a cold tap. Run the cold water onto it until the eggs are cool.

Tap the eggs on a hard surface to crack the shells. Peel the shells off. Cut the eggs in half lengthways.

Scoop the yolks into a bowl. Mash them up, stir in enough mayonnaise to make a stiff paste. Add salt and pepper.

Spoon the yolk mixture back onto the whites of the eggs and sprinkle a little chopped parsley on top.

Sausage rolls

INGREDIENTS

pastry made from:
60g (2½oz) margarine
  and 125g (4oz) plain
  flour (see page 24)
225g (8oz)
  sausagemeat
1 beaten egg

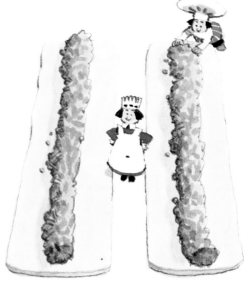

Oven setting: 220°C/435°F/
Gas mark 7
Grease a baking sheet.

Make the pastry (see page 24) and roll it out thinly into an oblong about 10cm (4in) wide. Cut it into two equal strips.

Cut the meat in half and roll it into two 'sausages' as long as the strips of pastry. Lay then down the centre of the pastry strips.

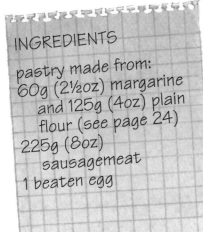

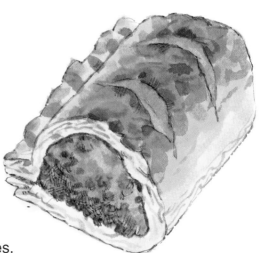

Brush the sides of the strips with egg. Fold one side of each strip over the sausagemeat and press the pastry edges firmly together.

Cut the rolls into small pieces. Brush them with beaten egg and cut two slits in the top of each one. Put them on a baking sheet.

Bake them for 20-25 minutes until golden brown.

Fish in breadcrumbs

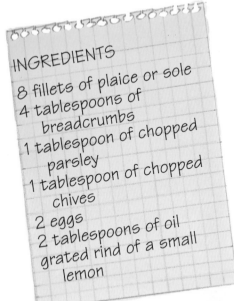

Beat the eggs in a shallow dish. Season them. Mix the herbs, breadcrumbs and lemon rind together in another shallow dish.

Pat the fillets of fish dry on kitchen paper. Dip them in the beaten egg then in the breadcrumbs, until evenly coated all over.

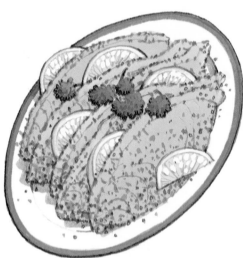

Heat the oil in a big frying pan. Fry the fillets for about three minutes on each side, until golden brown.

Take them out of the pan and drain them well on crumpled kitchen paper.

Serve the fish with wedges of lemon, boiled potatoes and a green salad.

Cheesy courgettes

INGREDIENTS

900g (2lb) courgettes
3 eggs
300 ml (½ pint) of single
    cream
125g (4oz) grated cheese
salt and black pepper
a pinch of nutmeg

Oven setting: 200°C/400°F/
Gas mark 6
Grease a shallow, ovenproof
baking dish.

Wash and slice the courgettes.
Cook in boiling, salted water for
three to four minutes, then drain.

Beat the eggs and cream
together in a bowl. Add the salt,
pepper and nutmeg.

You can eat
this with meat or as a
meal in itself.

Spread the courgettes over the bottom of the
baking dish. Pour the egg mixture over them
and sprinkle the grated cheese on top.

Bake the courgette for about 20 minutes, until the
egg mixture has set and the cheese is golden
brown and bubbly.

17

American burgers

INGREDIENTS

450g (1lb) minced beef
   or lamb
1 small chopped onion
a little beaten egg
salt and pepper
4 soft round rolls

Mix the meat, onion, egg, salt and pepper together in a bowl. Cut the rolls in half and toast the cut side.

Divide the mixture in four and use your hands to make each one into a burger shape.

Eat your burger with a baked potato, relishes and tomato ketchup.

Brush them with oil. Grill them under a high heat for six to ten minutes on each side.

Put each burger in a roll. You can add slices of cheese if you like, or lettuce, sliced tomatoes and mayonnaise.

Pork chops with apple

INGREDIENTS

4 pork chops
450g (1lb) onions
450g (1lb) cooking
    apples
1 tablespoon of sugar
salt and pepper
a knob of butter

Oven setting 180°C/350°F
Gas mark 4

Peel and slice the onions and apples. Spread the onions over the bottom of a casserole dish. Add a pinch of salt and pepper, then cover them with half the sliced apple and sprinkle with sugar.

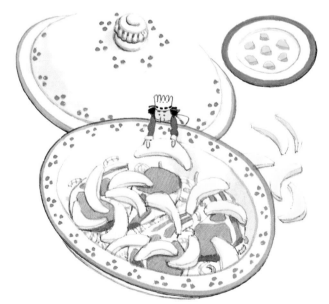

Put the pork chops in next. Add salt and pepper, then the rest of the apple and put a few dots of butter on top.

Put the lid on the casserole and bake the pork for 1-1½ hours until tender. Serve it with potatoes and a green vegetable.

Cheese soufflé

A soufflé looks impressive but is surprisingly easy to make. Soufflé means 'puffed up' in French. The soufflé puffs up and becomes lighter as it cooks because it contains whisked egg white, which has a lot of air in it.

INGREDIENTS

White sauce made from:
425 ml (¾ pint) milk
35g (1½oz) butter
30g (1½oz) plain flour
3 large eggs
85g (3½oz) grated cheese
salt and pepper
a pinch of nutmeg

Grease a 1½ pint (900ml) soufflé dish or pie dish.

Handy Tips
Use eggs that are at room temperature.

Stop whisking the egg whites as soon as they stand up in peaks.

Do not beat the mixture once you have folded in the egg whites.

Move one shelf to the centre of the oven and take out the shelves above it.
Oven setting: 190°C/375°F/ Gas mark 5

A soufflé starts to sink as soon as you take it out of the oven, so eat it straight away. Serve it with a green salad.

Separate the egg white from the yolk. Crack each egg over a bowl and slide the yolk from one half of the shell to the other.

The white will slip out of the shell into the bowl. Tip the yolk into another bowl. Beat the yolks together.

Make a white sauce following the steps on page 22. Stir in the nutmeg, grated cheese and egg yolks.

Whisk the egg whites until they form soft peaks. Stir a tablespoonful of them into the sauce, then gently fold in the rest. Do not beat the mixture or it will not rise.

Pour the mixture into the soufflé dish and put it in the oven. Bake it for 30-35 minutes until it is puffy and golden brown. Do not open the oven door while it is cooking.

Bacon and potato hotpot

INGREDIENTS

4 big onions
4 big potatoes
225g (8oz) bacon
425ml (¾ pint) milk
35g (1½oz) plain flour
35g (1½oz) butter
salt and pepper

Oven setting: 180°C/350°F/
Gas mark 4

Gently melt the butter in a saucepan. Add the flour and stir it until it bubbles.

Let the mixture cook for a minute, then take the pan off the heat and stir in the milk, a little at a time.

This page shows you how to make a white sauce. You make it before you start the hotpot, then pour it over the top.

Put the pan back on the heat. As the sauce gets hot it will thicken. Keep stirring so that it does not go lumpy. When the sauce boils, turn the heat down and let it simmer until it is thick and creamy. Season with salt and pepper and take it off the heat.

Now prepare everything else.

Peel and slice the potatoes and put them in cold water.

Peel the onions and chop them up as finely as you can.

Cut the rind off the bacon. Chop it into small bits.

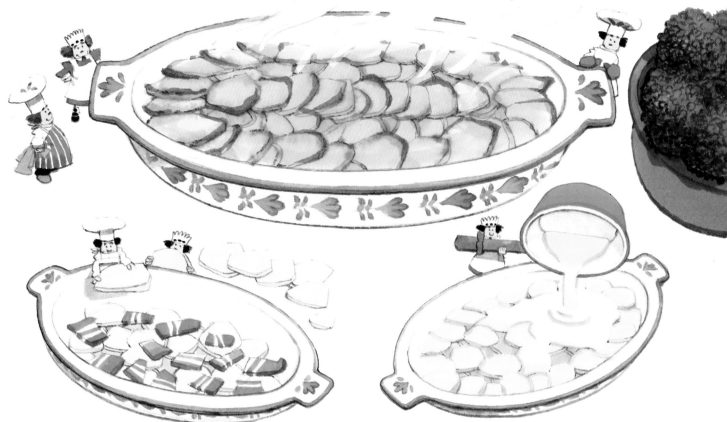

Grease an ovenproof dish and put in layers of potatoes, onions and bacon. Season each layer with salt and pepper. Repeat the layers, finishing with a layer of potatoes.

Pour the sauce on top and put the hotpot on the middle shelf of your oven. Bake it for about 1½ hours. Move it to the top shelf for the last 20 minutes so that the top browns.

Quiche Lorraine

INGREDIENTS
175g (6oz) plain flour
90g (3½oz) butter or
  margarine
3 tablespoons of cold water
a pinch of salt
For the filling:
6 rashers of bacon
300ml (½ pint) single cream
2 large eggs
salt and pepper
a pinch of nutmeg

'Quiche' is a French word for flan. The recipe for this bacon and cream flan comes from Lorraine in Eastern France.

Cut up the butter. Put it in a bowl with the flour and salt. Rub them together until they look like breadcrumbs.

Oven setting: 200°C/400°F/
Gas mark 6
Grease a 20cm (8in) flan dish or tin.

If the dough is crumbly, add more water; if it is sticky, add more flour. Sprinkle flour on a table and your rolling pin.

Sprinkle the water into the bowl. Mix the dough until it forms a soft ball that leaves the sides of the bowl clean.

Roll the pastry out thinly into a rough circle. Line the tin with it, prick it with a fork and trim off the edges.

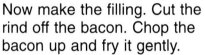

Now make the filling. Cut the rind off the bacon. Chop the bacon up and fry it gently.

Beat the eggs and cream in a bowl and season with salt, pepper and nutmeg.

Spread the bacon over the pastry and pour the egg mixture on top.

You can add lots of different things to quiche - grated cheese, mushrooms, leeks, tomatoes or onions.

Put the quiche in the oven and cook it for 30 minutes. It is done when the filling has set in the middle and is puffy and golden brown. You can eat it hot or cold. Serve it with a salad or green vegetables.

Spaghetti Bolognese

INGREDIENTS

450g (1lb) spaghetti
450g (1lb) minced beef
75g (3oz) bacon
2 onions
225g (8oz) tin of
    tomatoes
1 tablespoon of tomato
    purée
1 tablespoon of oil
1 clove of garlic
a pinch of basil
salt and pepper

The important thing to remember about cooking spaghetti is not to overcook it. It should be soft but still have a bit of 'bite' to it. Bolognese sauce is a meat and tomato sauce.

Peel and crush the garlic. Chop the onions finely.

Cut the rind of the bacon. Chop the bacon into small pieces.

Heat the oil in a big frying pan. Fry the garlic and onion gently until soft. Add the bacon and then the meat. Break it with fork and fry it, turning it until it is brown all over.

Add the tomatoes, purée, basil and a pinch of salt and pepper. Stir well, put a lid on the pan and simmer for 20 minutes.

Heat some water in a big pan. Add a pinch of salt and a teaspoon oil to it (this stops the spaghetti sticking together).

When the water is boiling, put the spaghetti in. Push it gently into the pan. It will slide down as the ends begin to soften.

Cook the spaghetti for eight to ten minutes until soft but not soggy. Then drain it well in a colander over your sink.

Put the spaghetti in a warm dish and pour the meat sauce on top. Mix it all together.

Serve the spaghetti with grated cheese to sprinkle on top and a green salad.

Perfect rice

INGREDIENTS
225g (8oz) long grain rice
600ml (1 pint) boiling water
1 tablespoon of oil
salt

Follow this recipe and you will have perfectly cooked fluffy rice every time.

Heat the oil in a saucepan. Add the rice, stir well and cook gently for a few minutes until it is transparent.

Add the water and salt. Put a lid on the pan and let the rice simmer. Do not stir it while it is cooking.

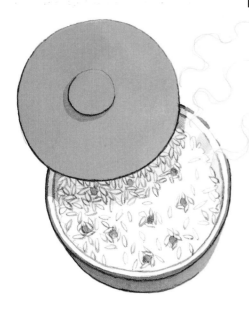

After 15 minutes (or 40 minutes, if you have brown rice), have a look. It should have absorbed all the water in the pan.

Bite a few grains to test if it is done. They should be tender. If still hard, add a little water and cook the rice a bit longer.

When the rice is done, spoon it into a warm serving dish and fluff it up with the prongs of a fork.

Risotto

Make this sauce while you cook the rice, then stir it into the rice to make a risotto.

INGREDIENTS

225g (8oz) cooked rice
1 red pepper
125g (4oz) mushrooms
2 tablespoons of tomato purée
2 onions
2 tablespoons of oil
6 rashers of bacon
4 tomatoes
125g (4oz) peas

Skin the tomatoes (see page 4) and chop them up. Wash and slice the mushrooms. Peel and chop the onions. Core the pepper and cut it into shreds. Cut the rind off the bacon and chop the bacon up into small pieces.

Heat the oil in a saucepan and cook the onion and bacon until the onion is soft. Add the other vegetables and tomato purée. Stir them well, then put a lid on the pan and let the vegetables cook slowly in their juices for 15-20 minutes.

Mix the rice and vegetables together in a saucepan, heat them up and then serve the risotto in a warm dish.

Chicken with lemon

INGREDIENTS

4 skinned chicken
   breasts
juice of half a lemon
juice of a big orange
1 tablespoon of soy sauce
butter
salt and pepper
clear honey

Oven setting: 150°C/300°F/
Gas mark 2
Grease a shallow baking tray.

Rub a spoonful of honey onto each chicken breast and lay them in a baking dish.

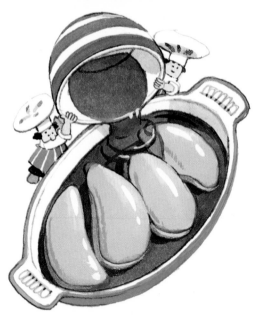

Mix the orange and lemon juice and soy sauce together. Season with salt and pepper and pour it over the chicken.

Cover the baking dish with foil and bake the chicken for about 40 minutes.

Push a skewer into the chicken to test if it is cooked. No pink juice should run out.

Serve the chicken with the sauce poured over it. Eat it with rice.

Kebabs

Cut the lambs into cubes. Put it in a bowl. Mix in the lemon, oil, salt, pepper and herbs to make a sauce called a marinade.

Peel the onion. Cut it into quarters, then separate the layers. Cut the tomatoes into quarters. Wash the mushrooms.

Drain the meat, then push everything together tightly on the skewers. Be careful of the sharp points.

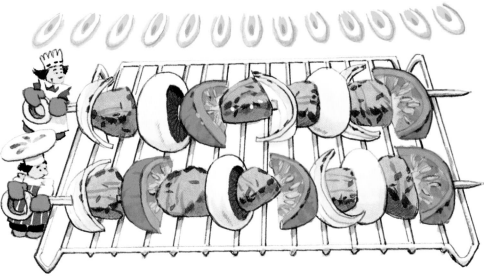

Put on oven gloves and grill the kebabs for about ten minutes. Turn them from time to time so they cook all over. They are done when the meat is brown on the outside but still juicy in the middle. Serve the kebabs with rice and a green salad.

Pizza

Bread dough takes a long time to rise, so start making it two and a half hours before you want to eat the pizza. Grease two 20cm (8in) flan tins.

INGREDIENTS
225g (8oz) plain flour
1 teaspoon salt
2 level teaspoons dried yeast
½ teaspoon sugar
75-150ml (⅛-¼ pint) hand hot water
1 medium tin tomatoes
1 tablespoon tomato purée
1 teaspoon dried herbs
125g (4oz) grated cheese
salt and pepper

Oven setting: 230°C/450°F/ Gas mark 8

Put two tablespoons of warm water in a jug and mix in the sugar and yeast. Put the jug in a warm place for ten minutes, until frothy.

Sift the flour and salt into a bowl. Mix in the yeast then just enough warm water to make a soft ball of dough that leaves the bowl clean.

Put the dough on a floured table and knead it for about five minutes. Push it away from you with one hand, gather it into a ball, turn and repeat.

When the dough is smooth and stretchy, put it in a greased bowl, cover it and put it in a warm place for about an hour.

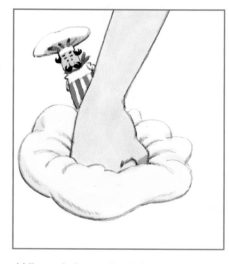

When it has doubled in size, take it out of the bowl and knead it for five more minutes. Split it into two balls and put each one in a flan tin.

Press the balls of dough out with your hands so they fill the tins. Pinch around the edges to make a border.

Drain the tomatoes and rub them through a sieve into a bowl. Stir in the tomato purée, salt and pepper.

Spread the tomato sauce over the pizzas, leaving the rims clear. Sprinkle the cheese and herbs on top.

Bake the pizzas on the middle shelf of the oven for 20-25 minutes until crisp and brown around the edges.

Eat the pizza hot. Cut it into wedges and serve it with salad. You can vary the toppings by adding strips of ham and bacon, sliced mushrooms, sliced sausages, olives or anchovies.

Juicy mixed salad

INGREDIENTS

½ crisp lettuce
¼ cucumber
2 tomatoes
2 sticks of celery
2 carrots
1 eating apple
a handful of nuts
1 tablespoon of chopped chives
1 tablespoon of chopped parsley

Shred the lettuce in your fingers.

Dice the cucumber.

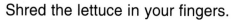

Chop the tomatoes, celery, carrots and apple.

BASIC DRESSING

3 tablespoons of oil
1 tablespoon of vinegar
a pinch of mustard
salt and black pepper
a pinch of sugar

Put everything into a screwtop jar and shake it well.

Mix all the vegetables in a large bowl. Ten minutes before you serve the salad, pour on the dressing and toss it.

Potato salad

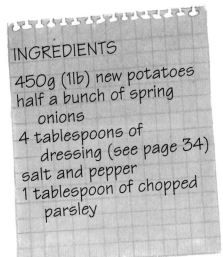

Scrub the potatoes and cook them in boiling water for 10-15 minutes until tender.

Drain them well.

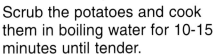

Clean and trim the spring onions. Chop them finely.

When the potatoes have cooled, chop them roughly.

Put them in a salad bowl with the onion. Pour the dressing on the salad and mix it gently. Sprinkle the parsley on top.

Apple crumble

INGREDIENTS
900g (2lb) cooking apples
50g (2oz) soft brown
 sugar
½ teaspoon of ground
 cinnamon
2 tablespoons of orange
 juice
For the crumble:
175g (6oz) plain flour
50g (2oz) sugar
75g (3oz) butter
a pinch of salt

You can make a crumble with any fruit you like. Try plums, raspberries or blackcurrants.

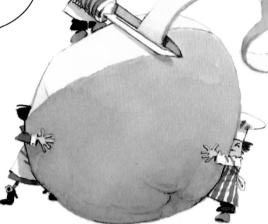

Peel the apples.

Oven setting: 200°C/400°F/
Gas mark 6

Cut the apples in half, cut out the cores and slice them.

Cook them in a saucepan with the orange juice, cinnamon and brown sugar until soft.

Pour the cooked apples into a 1 litre (2 pint) pie dish and spread them out evenly.

Making the crumble

Sift the flour and salt into a mixing bowl. Add the butter and cut it into small bits with a knife.

Rub the butter into the flour with your fingertips. Keep lifting you hands high above the bowl. This lets the air into the mixture and makes it light. Carry on until you have an even, crumbly mixture, then stir in the sugar.

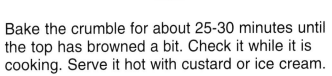

Spoon the crumble over the apples in the pie dish. Spread it out with a fork but do not press it down.

Bake the crumble for about 25-30 minutes until the top has browned a bit. Check it while it is cooking. Serve it hot with custard or ice cream.

Summer fruit pudding

INGREDIENTS

225g (8oz) strawberries
125g (4oz) raspberries
2 peaches
2 bananas
1 pear
1 orange
½ lemon
castor sugar

You can put any fruit you like in your fruit salad.

You can make this juicy salad with any fresh fruit that is in season.

Squeeze the juice out of the orange and lemon and pour it into a serving bowl.

Core and slice the pear and put it in the bowl. Peel the banana and slice it into the bowl. Gently stir the fruit in the orange and lemon juice. This stops it from turning brown.

Cut the peaches in half and take out the stones.

Peel and slice the peaches. Wash and pat dry the strawberries and raspberries.

Take the stalks out of the strawberries and cut any big strawberries in half.

Put the peaches, strawberries and raspberries in the bowl. Sprinkle a little sugar over the fruit and gently mix it together. Put it in the fridge to chill for an hour or so.

You can add any of these things to a fruit salad: plums, cherries, pineapples, apples, apricots, oranges, grapes.

Juicy oranges

INGREDIENTS

6 oranges
1 lemon
2 tablespoons of
    sugar

Peel four oranges and cut off the pith. Slice them and take out the pips.

Grate the peel off the lemon. Squeeze out the juice of half the lemon.

You could eat these oranges with crème fraîche or ice cream.

Put the sliced oranges in a dish and sprinkle the sugar and lemon peel over them. Squeeze out the juice of the other two oranges.

Pour the juice from the oranges and lemon over the oranges. Mix them gently and put them in the fridge to chill.

Pear flan

INGREDIENTS

5 pears
125g (4oz) butter
125g (4oz) flour
125g (4oz) caster
    sugar
3 eggs
a pinch of salt
a few drops of vanilla
    essence

Oven setting: 180°C/350°F/
Gas mark 4
Grease an ovenproof flan dish.

Melt the butter in a saucepan over a low heat.

Beat the eggs and sugar together. Stir in the butter, then the flour, a little at a time. Add the vanilla essence and a pinch of salt.

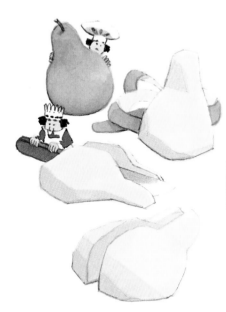

Peel the pears and cut them into quarters. Cut out the cores and any pips.

Pour a little mixture into the dish. Put in the pears, then the rest of the mixture.

Bake the flan for 45 minutes to an hour until it is puffy and golden brown.

Lemon cheesecake

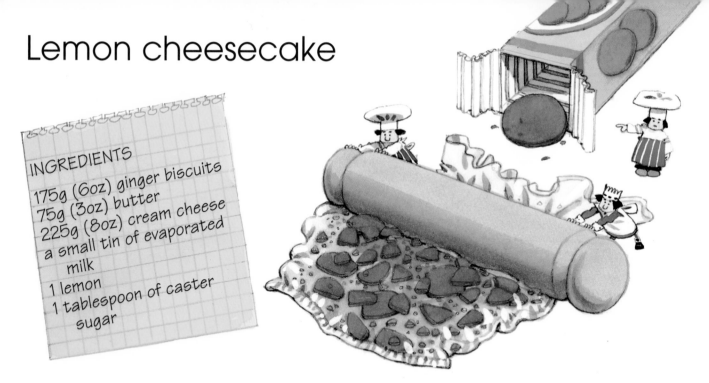

INGREDIENTS

175g (6oz) ginger biscuits
75g (3oz) butter
225g (8oz) cream cheese
a small tin of evaporated
  milk
1 lemon
1 tablespoon of caster
  sugar

Grease a 20cm (8 inch) flan dish or tin, well.

Break the biscuits into a plastic bag and crush them into fine crumbs with a rolling pin.

Melt the butter in a saucepan over a low heat. Add the crumbs and stir well.

Press the mixture evenly into the flan dish or tin. Put it in the fridge. It hardens as it chills.

Grate the lemon rind. Then cut the lemon in half and squeeze out all the juice.

Put the cream cheese in a big bowl and beat it with a wooden spoon to make it soft. Add the evaporated milk a little at a time, beating all the while to make a smooth mixture.

Quickly stir in the sugar, lemon rind and juice.

When the mixture is smooth, pour it over the biscuit base. Level it with a knife.

Cover the cheesecake with foil and put it in the fridge to chill for at least three hours. When it has set, decorate it with grated chocolate or twists of lemon peel.

Pancakes

INGREDIENTS

225g (8oz) plain flour
a pinch of salt
300ml (½ pint) milk
and 300ml (½ pint)
water, mixed

1 egg
1 tablespoon of melted
butter

Sift the flour and salt into a big mixing bowl. Hold the sieve up high so that lots of air gets into the flour.

Make a hollow in the flour and break in the eggs. Whisk them, drawing in some flour from the sides.

You can leave the mixture until you are ready to use it, but stir it well before making your pancakes.

Add the water and milk mixture a bit at time. Keep whisking and drawing in the flour until everything is mixed together.

Add the melted butter. Beat the mixture until it is smooth and just thick enough to coat a wooden spoon.

44

Melt a little butter in a frying pan and swirl it around. Pour half a cup of the mixture, or batter as it is called, into the pan.

Quickly tilt the pan in all directions until a thin layer of batter covers the base.

Cook the pancake until bubbles appear and the edges turn brown. Flip it over and cook it on the other side.

Slip the pancake onto a warm plate, sprinkle it with lemon juice and sugar and roll it up. Then start on the next one.

Eat pancakes while they are hot. When you have a party it is fun to pass them to your friends as you make them. You can spread pancakes with warmed jam or honey if you like.

Profiteroles

Profiteroles are light, puffy little buns made of choux pastry. You make the pastry in a saucepan.

Oven setting: 200°C/400°F/ Gas mark 6
Grease a baking sheet and dampen it by holding it under a cold tap for a few seconds.

Cut up the butter and heat it in a saucepan with the water.
Sift the flour on to a sheet of greaseproof paper.

When the mixture in the pan starts to boil, take it off the heat and pour all the flour into the mixture in one go.

Beat the mixture until it is smooth and comes away easily from the sides of the pan. This only takes a minute.

Cool the mixture for about five minutes then beat in the egg a bit at a time to make a thick, smooth, glossy paste.

Put teaspoons of pastry on the baking sheet and put it in the oven. After ten minutes turn the temperature up to 220°C/425°F/ Gas mark 7.

46

Bake for another 15-20 minutes, then peep into the oven. The buns should look puffy and golden brown.

Put them onto a wire rack. Prick a hole in the side of each one with the point of a knife to let out any steam.

Put the chocolate and water in a bowl. Heat gently over a pan of water until the chocolate melts. Stir it until it's smooth, then put it aside.

Whip the cream. Make a hole in the side of each profiterole and fill them with a teaspoonful of cream.

Pile the profiteroles onto a serving plate and pour the chocolate sauce over them.

47

Strawberry tarts

INGREDIENTS

175g (6oz) sifted plain
    flour
85g (3½oz) butter
85g (3½oz) caster sugar
3 egg yolks, beaten
a pinch of salt
450g (1lb) strawberries
175g (6oz) redcurrant
    jelly

Oven setting: 200°C/400°F/
Gas mark 6

Rub the flour, sugar, salt and butter together in a bowl until they look like breadcrumbs (see page 37).

Add the egg yolks. Mix well with a knife, then work the mixture with your hands to make a smooth ball of dough.

The dough should be soft but not sticky. Add some water if it is dry or more flour if it is sticky. If you put it in the fridge for 30 minutes it is easier to roll out.

Roll out the pastry until it is quite thin. Use a cutter to stamp out rounds of pastry and press them into tart tins.

Prick the pastry with a fork and line with greaseproof paper. Put in dry beans or rice. This stops them from puffing up.

48

Making glaze

Bake the pastry for 15 minutes, then take out the paper and beans. Bake them for five more minutes, until light brown, then cool them on a wire rack.

Make a glaze for the tarts by melting the redcurrant jelly in a small pan over a low heat.

Wash the strawberries and take out the stalks. Cut any big strawberries in half.

When the pastry cases are cool, brush the insides with a thick coat of redcurrant glaze. Arrange the strawberries in the cases and brush them with more glaze. It sets as it cools.

Other fruit tarts

You can fill tarts with grapes, raspberries, gooseberries or apricots too.

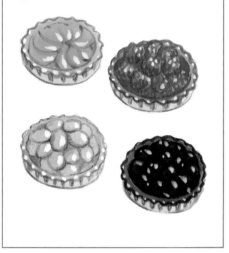

49

Chocolate mousse

INGREDIENTS

125g (4oz) plain chocolate

4 eggs

1 tablespoon of water

Break the chocolate into a bowl. Add a tablespoonful of water. Heat some water in a saucepan and let it simmer.

Stand the bowl over the pan. When the chocolate melts, stir it until smooth, then put it to one side to cool.

Be careful not to mix any egg yolk in with the whites, or you will not be able to whisk the whites properly.

Separate the egg whites from the yolks. To do this you need two bowls. Crack each egg over one of the bowls, then slip the yolk from one half of the shell to the other. The white will slip into the bowl below. Put the yolk in the other bowl.

Beat the egg yolks until smooth, then slowly stir them into the chocolate.

Add a pinch of salt to the egg whites and whisk them until they stand up in peaks.

Gently fold the egg whites into the chocolate mixture, using metal spoon. Cut into the mixture and turn it over lightly until it is evenly mixed. Do not beat it.

Carefully pour the mousse into a serving dish and put it in the fridge for a few hours. When it has set, sprinkle grated chocolate over it. Serve it with cream.

Ice cream sundaes

You can have great fun making ice cream sundaes. You need different flavours of ice cream, some sauces, chopped nuts, fruit and grated chocolate. Here are some ideas to try.

mixed ices with chocolate sauce

coffee icecream with toffee sauce

vanilla icecream sliced banana and raspberry sauce

vanilla icecream pears and chocolate sauce

Chocolate sauce

125g (4oz) plain chocolate
3 tablespoons of water

Break the chocolate into bits and put it in a small basin with the water.

Stand this over a pan of simmering water until the chocolate melts. Stir well.

Raspberry sauce

225g (8oz) raspberries
4 tablespoons of castor sugar

Wash the raspberries then press them through a nylon sieve into a bowl.

Stir in the sugar a spoonful at a time and beat well until the sugar has dissolved.

Toffee sauce

25g (1oz) butter or margarine
75g (3oz) brown sugar
2 tablespoons of golden syrup
4 tablespoons of cream

Put the butter, sugar and syrup in a small pan. Heat them gently until they melt.

Add the cream and stir everything together. Serve the sauce hot or cold.

Muesli

INGREDIENTS

125g (4oz) porridge oats
1 tablespoon wheatgerm
50g (2oz) raisins
50g (2oz) chopped nuts
2 apples
2 small cartons of natural
     yogurt
honey or brown sugar

"Eat muesli for breakfast. It will give you lots of energy."

Mix the oats, wheatgerm, raisins, nuts and yogurt together in a big bowl. Peel, core and grate the apples, then stir them quickly into the muesli so that they do not go brown.

You can make lots of muesli and keep it in a storage jar. Spoon it out into bowls and add the apple and yogurt when you are ready to eat it.

Add what you like to your muesli - milk, a teaspoon of honey or some brown sugar.

You can try sliced banana with it or strawberries. Peaches taste good too.

Banana and honey whip

INGREDIENTS

4 ripe bananas
small carton of whipping cream
1½ small cartons of plain yogurt
2 tablespoons of clear honey
a handful of flaked almonds
a squeeze of lemon juice

Whip the cream in a bowl until it is light and fluffy.

Peel and slice the bananas into another bowl. Mash them with a fork.

Stir the yogurt, honey and lemon juice into the banana.

Fold in the whipped cream. Spoon into serving dishes.

Sprinkle the almonds on top.

Raisin flapjacks

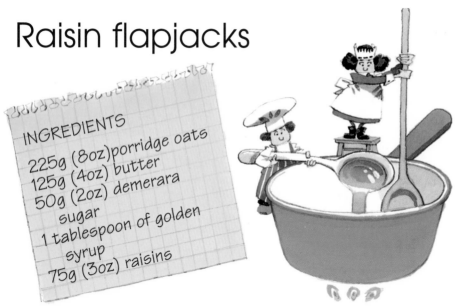

INGREDIENTS

225g (8oz) porridge oats
125g (4oz) butter
50g (2oz) demerara
    sugar
1 tablespoon of golden
    syrup
75g (3oz) raisins

Oven setting: 180°C/350°F/
Gas mark 4
Grease a shallow, oblong tin
18 x 28cm (7 x 11 inches)

Melt the butter, sugar and
syrup together over a very low
heat. Stir them together with a
wooden spoon.

Take the pan off the heat.
Add the oats and raisins to the
mixture and stir everything
together well.

Pour the mixture into the
baking tin and press it down.
Bake it for 20 minutes.

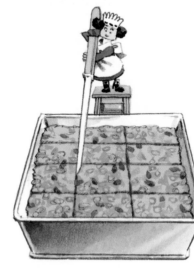

Cut the flapjacks into squares.
When they are cool take them
out of the baking tin. Store
them in a biscuit tin.

Chocolate brownies

INGREDIENTS

125g (4oz) plain chocolate
125g (4oz) butter
225g (8oz) castor
    sugar
2 beaten eggs
125g (4oz) plain flour
½ teaspoon baking powder
125g (4oz) chopped walnuts
a pinch of salt

Oven setting: 180°C/350°F/
Gas mark 4
Grease a shallow oblong tin
18 x 28cm (7 x 11 inches)

Break the chocolate up into a bowl and add the butter. Put the bowl over a saucepan of gently simmering water.

When the butter and chocolate have melted, take the bowl off the heat and stir in all the other ingredients.

Brownies are crisp on top and gooey in the middle.

Spread the mixture into the baking tin and put it in the oven to bake for 30 minutes.

Let the mixture cool in the tin for 10 minutes. It will sink a little bit. Then cut the brownies into squares and cool them on a wire rack. Store them in a biscuit tin.

Marmalade gingerbread

Use chunky marmalade for this recipe.

INGREDIENTS
225g (8oz) self-raising
 flour
1 beaten egg
75g (3oz) butter or
 margarine
1 teaspoon of ground
 cinnamon
2 teaspoons of ground
 ginger
150g (5oz) golden syrup
225g (8oz) marmalade
1 tablespoon of hot water
a pinch of salt

Oven setting: 170°C/325°F/
Gas mark 3

Grease a 18cm (7in) square
cake in. Line it with
baking parchment, as below.

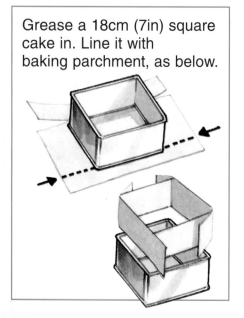

Cut up the butter. Put it in a saucepan with the syrup. Melt them over a low heat.

Sift the flour, ginger, salt and cinnamon into a bowl. Make a hollow in the centre.

Slowly pour the syrup mixture into the hollow, stirring in the flour from the sides as you do so. Add the marmalade, egg and water and mix everything together.

The mixture should be soft and drop off a spoon easily. If it is stiff, add more water.

Pour the mixture into the cake tin and spread it out evenly with a knife.

Bake the cake on the centre shelf of the oven for an hour.

The cake is done when it is golden brown and the centre feels springy to the touch. If you push a skewer into the centre of the cake it should come out clean.

Let the cake cool in the tin for 15 minutes then turn it out on to a wire cooling rack.

The cake lasts well if you put it in a tin.

Fudge

INGREDIENTS

450g (1lb) soft brown sugar
50g (2 oz) butter or margarine
275ml (½ pint) milk
a few drops of vanilla essence

Be very careful not to let the fudge boil over!

Grease a baking tin 15 x 15cm (6 x 6in)

Boiling sugar is dangerous. Do not make fudge unless there is an adult to help you.

Heat the sugar, butter and milk in a saucepan until the sugar dissolves. Bring to the boil, stirring all the time. Boil for about thirty minutes.

Drip a little fudge onto a bowl of cold water. It will form a soft ball when it is done. Keep boiling and testing until it does this.

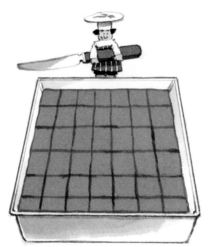

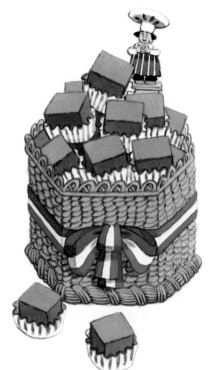

Take the pan off the heat, add the vanilla and beat the mixture until thick and creamy. Pour it into the tin.

Leave it to set, then cut into squares. You can make other sorts of fudge by adding cocoa, nuts or raisins.

Meringues

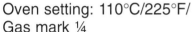

INGREDIENTS

4 egg whites*
225g (8oz) sifted
caster sugar

Oven setting: 110°C/225°F/
Gas mark ¼

Brush two baking sheets with oil and sift a little flour on top. Tap them on a table to spread the flour out evenly.

Whisk the egg whites in a big bowl until stiff. Add half the sugar, a spoonful at a time, whisking all the time.

Very gently fold the rest of the sugar into the egg whites, using a metal spoon.

Drop spoonfuls of the mixture on the baking sheets, 3 cm (1in) apart. Shape them into rounds.

Bake the meringues for 2-2½ hours until they are set and a pale honey colour. Put them on a wire rack to cool.

You can eat your meringues on their own or sandwich them together with whipping cream.

*See page 50 - for how to separate eggs. You could use the yolks to make strawberry tarts.

Fruit cake

INGREDIENTS

225g (8oz) plain flour
1 teaspoon of baking
    powder
1 teaspoon of mixed spice
175g (6oz) soft brown
    sugar
175g (6oz) butter
3 medium eggs, beaten
125g (4oz) currants
125g (4oz) raisins
125g (4oz) sultanas
50g (2oz) glace cherries
50g (2oz) mixed peel
50g (2oz) ground almonds
50g (2oz) blanched
    almonds

Oven setting: 140°C/275°F/
Gas mark 1

It is easier to make the cake if you take the butter and eggs out of the fridge an hour before you start.

1. Cut a strip of baking parchment long enough to go around a 18-20cm (7-8in) round cake tin.

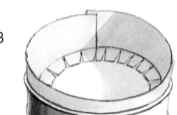

2. Fold back 2cm (¾in) all the way along it and snip it like this.

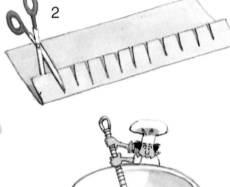

Grease the tin all over the inside with butter.

3. Press the strip around the inside of the tin.

4. Cut out a circle of paper to line the base.

Beat the eggs.

Rinse and dry the glace cherries and cut them in half.

Put the butter and sugar in a mixing bowl and beat them together with a wooden spoon until they are fluffy.

Mix the eggs a bit at a time. Then gently fold in the baking powder and flour. The mixture should drop easily off a spoon.

Add a little milk to the cake mixture if it seems too stiff. Using a tablespoon, carefully fold in the dried fruit. Then gently fold in the cherries, salt, mixed spice, mixed peel and ground almonds. Do not beat the cake mixture.

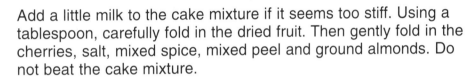

Spoon the mixture into the tin and smooth it out on top. Gently arrange the almonds on top of the cake.

Bake the cake in the centre of the oven for 2-2½ hours. It is done when the centre feels firm and springy to the touch. If you stick a skewer in it should come out clean. Let the cake cool before you take it out of the tin.

Iced spice biscuits

INGREDIENTS
225g (8oz) plain flour
125g (4oz) butter
125g (4oz) brown sugar
1 small beaten egg
2 teaspoons of mixed
    spice
pinch of salt
For the icing:
125g (4oz) icing sugar
1-2 tablespoons hot water
food colouring

Oven setting: 190°C/375°F/
Gas mark 5
Grease two baking trays.

Beat the butter and sugar together until fluffy. Beat in the egg a bit at a time.

Sift the flour, salt and spice. Mix everything well to make a ball of firm dough.

Sprinkle some flour on a table and a rolling pin, then roll the dough out until it is about ½cm (¼in) thick.

Cut the dough into shapes. Gather up any dough left over, roll it out again and cut out more shapes.

Put the biscuits on the trays. Bake them on a high shelf in the oven for about fifteen minutes, until light brown.

Put the biscuits in a wire rack to cool. Mix the icing sugar and hot water together in a bowl until smooth.

Spoon the icing into two of three cups and add a drop of different food colouring to each one. Leave some white.

When the biscuits are cool, spoon half a teaspoon of icing onto each one and spread it out evenly.

Before the icing sets, decorate the biscuits with silver balls or anything else you like.

Special chocolate cake

INGREDIENTS
175g (6oz) plain chocolate
175g (6oz) soft butter
175g (6oz) caster sugar
4 beaten egg yolks
4 egg whites
90g (3½oz) ground
    almonds
90g (3½oz) plain flour
Chocolate fudge Icing:
75g (3oz) sugar
50g (2oz) butter or
    margarine
125g (4oz) plain chocolate
75 ml (3floz) evaporated
    milk

Oven setting: 180°C/350°F/
Gas mark 4

Break the chocolate into a bowl. Stand it over a pan of simmering water until the chocolate melts. Stir well.

Cream the butter and sugar until fluffy. Beat in the egg yolks, bit by bit. Stir in the chocolate and almonds.

Whisk the egg whites in a big bowl until they form soft peaks. Do not go on beating them or they will collapse.

Do not beat the mixture.

Gently fold some egg white then some flour into the cake mixture. Carry on until you have used them both up.

Grease two 20 cm (8 inch) sandwich tins.

Spread the mixture into the tins. Bake for 20 minutes, until the centres of the cakes feel springy.

Leave the cakes in the tins for a few minutes, then slip a knife around the sides and turn them on to a wire rack.

While the cake bakes, make the icing. Heat the evaporated milk and sugar in a pan. Stir and bring to the boil, then let the sauce simmer for five minutes.

Take the pan off the heat. Add the broken-up chocolate and stir until it has melted. Do the same with the butter.

Pour the icing into the bowl, When cool, put it in the fridge. It thickens as it cools and becomes easier to spread.

When the cake and icing are cool, spread half the icing on top of the cake. Put the other cake on top and spread the rest of the icing over it.

Handy hints

Mixing

Use a wooden spoon to mix ingredients together, to stir things in a pan and to add eggs or egg yolks to a mixture.

Beating eggs

Beat eggs with a whisk or fork until they are mixed and frothy. Stand the bowl on a damp cloth to stop it from sliding about.

Whisking eggs

Whisk egg whites until they form soft peaks. If you whisk them for too long they go lumpy and will not fold into the mixture properly.

Greasing a tin

Put a tiny piece of butter or margarine on some kitchen paper and rub it round inside the tin until it is lightly greased all over.

Icing a cake

To spread icing easily, use a rounded knife dipped in warm water to smooth the icing over the top and sides of the cake.

Looking good

Always make things look nice before you serve them. Decorate cakes or puddings with lemon or orange twists.

Preparing vegetables

Wash vegetables quickly but well in cold water. Do not soak them for too long. If they are gritty, scrub them clean with a brush used for cooking.

Peel carrots and potatoes if they are big. Little, new ones need only be washed or scraped with a knife.

Cut any tough stalks, wilted leaves, tops and tails off green vegetables then chop or slice them as in the picture.

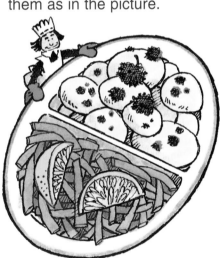

Boil a little salted water in a pan. Cook the vegetables with the lid on until tender but still a bit crunchy. Do not overcook them.

Stick a skewer into vegetables to test if they are done. Then tip them into a colander over a sink and drain them well.

Serve vegetables hot, tossed in butter. Garnish them with chopped parsley, sprigs of parsley or wedges of lemon.

Cooking things

frying pan

saucepan

wire rack

rolling pin

chopping board

cake tin

flan tin

mixing bowl

measuring jug

colander

whisks (egg beater, wire whisk)

sieve

timer

potato peeler

metal slice

ovenproof casserole

pastry brush

lemon squeezer

scales

pepper grinder

palette knife

tin opener

garlic press

pastry cutters

spatula

grater

kitchen scissors

baking tray

kitchen knives (1 big, 1 serrated, 1 small - all sharp)

Cooking words

BAKE — Cook in an oven.

BEAT — Mix by stirring vigorously with a fork, a wooden spoon or a whisk.

BOIL — Cook in boiling water.

BRING TO THE BOIL — Heat a liquid until it starts to boil.

CREAM — Beat butter and sugar together with a wooden spoon.

FOLD IN — Gently mix an ingredient into a creamed mixture, using a metal spoon.

FRY — Cook in hot fat or oil.

GARNISH — Decorate food with things such as chopped parsley.

GLAZE — Coat food with beaten egg, milk or melted jam, to make it look shiny.

GREASE — Rub the inside of a baking tin or ovenproof dish with butter or margarine, to stop food from sticking to it.

GRILL — Cook food under a grill.

KNEAD — Work a dough firmly with your hands on a flat surface until it's smooth and stretchy.

MARINADE — A mixture in which you soak meat or fish before cooking it, to make it tender and to give it flavour.

SEPARATE AN EGG — To divide the egg white from the yolk.

SIFT — Shake flour or icing sugar through a sieve, to get rid of lumps and make it light.

RUB IN — Rub fat into flour with your fingertips until the mixture looks like breadcrumbs.

SEASON — Add salt, pepper or herbs to food to give it more flavour.

SIMMER — Cook a liquid over a low heat so that it is just bubbling, but not boiling.

WHISK — Beat vigorously with a whisk, to add air to a mixture and make it light.

71

Index